# ELSBETH

# Vivian Quinn and the Dying World

*Copyright © 2023 by Elsbeth*

*All rights reserved. No part of this publication may be reproduced, stored or transmitted in any form or by any means, electronic, mechanical, photocopying, recording, scanning, or otherwise without written permission from the publisher. It is illegal to copy this book, post it to a website, or distribute it by any other means without permission.*

*This novel is entirely a work of fiction. The names, characters and incidents portrayed in it are the work of the author's imagination. Any resemblance to actual persons, living or dead, events or localities is entirely coincidental.*

*Elsbeth asserts the moral right to be identified as the author of this work.*

*Elsbeth has no responsibility for the persistence or accuracy of URLs for external or third-party Internet Websites referred to in this publication and does not guarantee that any content on such Websites is, or will remain, accurate or appropriate.*

*Designations used by companies to distinguish their products are often claimed as trademarks. All brand names and product names used in this book and on its cover are trade names, service marks, trademarks and registered trademarks of their respective owners. The publishers and the book are not associated with any product or vendor mentioned in this book. None of the companies referenced within the book have endorsed the book.*

*First edition*

*This book was professionally typeset on Reedsy. Find out more at reedsy.com*

*This book is dedicated to all those who struggle with mental illness and unresolved trauma.
I know that the task can seem daunting, but if you want to get better, help is out there waiting.*

# Contents

| | |
|---|---|
| *Acknowledgement* | ii |
| Chapter 1 | 1 |
| Chapter 2 | 11 |
| Chapter 3 | 21 |
| Chapter 4 | 29 |
| Chapter 5 | 39 |
| Chapter 6 | 47 |
| *About the Author* | 56 |
| *Also by Elsbeth* | 57 |

# Acknowledgement

Thank you to my editors, proofreaders, and cover artists, including Paul, Ira, and Jake Lee. Without your insight, this story wouldn't be in the great shape that it's in today.

# Chapter 1

As a small spaceship made its way toward a colossal planet, a young woman put down the small analog device she was holding onto her bed and stood up.

From the front of the ship, an expressive robotic voice said, "Vivian, are you there?"

Vivian Quinn returned to the cockpit and called out to her ship's flight computer, "Yeah, EVA. I'm here. What's our status?"

"Landing at three dot zero dot zero five."

"Affirmative," she said, sitting in the pilot seat and strapping herself in.

The planet's size took up the entire view from the front window of the tiny ship, and Vivian took a moment to take in the sight in front of her.

"Do we know anything about this place?"

"Oxygen-nitrogen atmosphere, turbulent weather."

"Is it safe to breathe?"

"Barometric pressure is close to nominal, you should be okay."

"Right," Vivian said. "Is there anything else I should know about this place?"

"Stand by," EVA said, a whirring noise occurring inside the

dashboard.

EVA, standing for Engineered Vehicle Aviator, was Vivian's built-in flight computer. Sometimes, Vivian had a hard time physically connecting with her, but she was so integrated into the ship itself that she could feel the ship tense up when EVA was overworked or stressed.

"Intangibility doesn't mean I don't care for you," EVA would always say on hard days.

After a minute, EVA responded, "Orbital period is 350 days, though approximately 280 of those days are spent in complete darkness."

Vivian felt anxiety develop in the pit of her stomach.

"Elaborate."

"The majority of the year is spent in eclipse. M101-865, designated as *Cephi*, is a moon that orbits the gas giant *Arvis*."

Vivian sighed and mumbled to herself, "Jackson, what have you gotten yourself into this time?"

"Pardon?"

Vivian replied, "Nothing, I'm just lamenting this mission."

"You volunteered to help," EVA said. "After all, you said Jackson was your friend."

"That's half the issue," Vivian said, her emotions a whirlwind just from the conversation. "I'm still upset about how we ended things."

"The way *you* ended things."

"Whatever," Vivian said, anger rising to the top of her emotional tornado.

"Vivian, I'm sure it will be okay."

Vivian sighed, zipping up her dark brown bomber jacket. "I just don't wanna see him again. You know what happened."

EVA responded, "It will be fine. It's simply a quick rescue

# CHAPTER 1

mission."

Before the conversation could continue, EVA changed tone and said, "Prepare for entry, descent, and landing."

As the ship approached the moon, Vivian looked out the main window and toward Arvis, seeing the swirling blues and oranges. The nuances of the elements' colors, combined with the planet's turbulent atmosphere laid a tapestry before Vivian that left her mesmerized.

"Activating retro-thrusters," EVA said as the ship bucked from the sudden decrease in velocity.

"Do we know where he is?"

"I extrapolated the data from his last certifiable transmission origin. Preparing for entry now."

Vivian could see the blue glow of Cephi's atmosphere quickly approaching, followed seconds later by the low rumble of the ship heating up.

As plasma licked off the snub-nosed ship, Vivian took off her jacket to cool down. While she always wore that jacket to hide her smallish frame from those who might want to hurt her, she was alone now, and she was sweating.

She put the jacket in her lap and looked through the canopy of the cockpit, seeing the atmosphere of the planet burn around her.

As the temperature rose, Vivian watched as the ship continued on its programmed trajectory.

"It's so hot in here," Vivian said, fanning herself. "Are thermal levels looking good?"

"All levels are within safe ranges," EVA responded as the rumble increased. "The thicker the atmosphere, the hotter it's gonna get."

"Well, what's a moon this small doing with an atmosphere

this thick?" Vivian asked, holding onto the seatbelt as beads of sweat dripped down her forehead.

"Unknown, there is no known ecological data on this world," EVA replied.

Just as EVA spoke, the heat started to subside.

Within seconds of the plasma dissipating, the ship passed through the cloud layer and Vivian could see a world teeming with botanical life, with some trees reaching over a hundred meters into the sky.

"It's beautiful!" She said, completely taken aback by the small moon's expansive and unexpected life.

*But I can't let it distract me,* Vivian thought as she refocused her attention on the mission at hand.

Vivian noticed a fairly large crater in the middle of the lush forest as she looked toward the surface.

"Is that where he landed?"

"Yes."

"He's a shit pilot," Vivian said, rolling her eyes.

"Affirmative."

Vivian grinned and looked at a small bonfire to the left of the still-smoldering crater.

"There," Vivian said. "Ten o'clock."

"Adjusting," EVA said.

The ship banked to the left as Vivian could hear the engines compensating for the speed lost during the turn.

"Let's try to land about 50 meters away."

"Affirmative," EVA said as it temporarily increased the thrust.

"Entering final descent."

The whirring of the airbrakes clicking into place startled Vivian for a moment before she said, "Let's aim for a vertical landing."

## CHAPTER 1

"Affirmative," EVA said.

The ship's thrusters reoriented as the ship groaned at the sudden movement and loss of speed.

Vivian put her hand back on the dashboard and watched the altimeter as it decreased in altitude and speed simultaneously until they hit zero at the same time. Vivian sighed, relieved that the landing went as well as it did.

As she threw her jacket back on, she noticed that the previously bright world was already darkening from another eclipse.

Vivian walked down the ramp and saw the vegetation recede as darkness took over the landscape, leaving the glow from Jackson's fire as the only light.

Her anxiety spiked, worried about what he might think of her, considering that she had previously pushed him away. She saw him wave to her and she started the short trek to his camp.

As she got close, she could see him adjusting his hair which had gotten tousled by the thrust of her ship's engines.

"Isn't it fascinating?" He asked.

"Hm?"

"The plants, they retreat when the darkness comes."

"Uh-huh," Vivian said.

"Have you heard the stories about this place? They say that demons roam this place in the darkness."

"Interesting," Vivian said, completely disinterested in what he was saying. "You have your stuff packed?"

Jackson sighed as he put out the fire and grabbed a case.

"Yeah, it's all packed. Seems like you haven't changed a bit."

Vivian grabbed the other bag and gestured toward her ship. "Let's get going."

Jackson and Vivian walked back to the ship and as they got inside, Vivian asked, "Where to?"

"Refueling Station 5, Sector 6. Not too far, all things considered."

"Make yourself comfortable, I guess," Vivian said, pointing to the two jumpseats in the main common area of the ship.

"It's smaller than I remember," Jackson said as he sat down in one of the jumpseats.

Vivian just scoffed as she hopped into the cockpit and relayed the information to EVA.

She stayed in the cockpit as they launched and pushed through the atmosphere and by the time they were nearing the jump point, Vivian had become less anxious and wandered out to the common area.

"How's *The Victory*?" Jackson asked, feigning genuine curiosity.

Vivian put her hand on the interior hull.

"I'd say it's holding up pretty well since I made some, uh, *modifications* to it."

Jackson nervously chuckled as Vivian paused while she pondered her next words.

"If I may ask, what's at Refueling Station 5, Sector 6?" She asked, tentatively.

"I have a huge carrier out there, I bought it for cheap and I'm planning on renting out space in it to anyone who needs a place in the sector."

"That's... a choice," Vivian said, chuckling at the idea. "Where are you headed with it?"

"Planning on going to Sector 3, seeing if anyone wants in on my project. How about you, where are you headed next?"

"Dunno," Vivian said, shrugging, then sarcastically said, "Wherever people need me, I guess."

Jackson nodded and said, "I respect that, it's... admirable."

## CHAPTER 1

"Thanks," Vivian said, not wanting to tell Jackson how she actually felt.

Vivian changed her tone slightly and said, "Getting all the way out here was a pain, you know?"

"Yeah," Jackson responded, opening up a small canteen of water. "I can imagine."

*Can't this bastard say thank you?* Vivian thought, then faked a smile.

Jackson didn't notice and said, "I've heard the nutrition out here is really good."

"Yeah? I was hoping that the stores out here carry something different."

The conversation lulled as Jackson nodded.

Vivian started to turn around to go back to the cockpit when Jackson asked, "Have you been seeing anyone recently?"

Vivian felt the pit in her stomach return and she shook her head.

"I heard that you were dating Rigel, are you two still in touch?"

Vivian sighed, "I've been trying to avoid him, actually."

"Why's that? You get attached too quickly and then break up?"

Vivian leaned forward and nervously nodded, saying, "Yep, you know it."

Jackson laughed and said, "You gotta stop doing that, it's not helping you."

"Please, don't," Vivian said as she stood up, her anger building as she rose.

"I'm only trying to help-"

"I don't want your help. Saving your ungrateful ass was stressful enough. I don't need *you* to tell me why I'm a failure."

Jackson put his hands up in self-defense.

"I didn't mean to say anything wrong-"

"You *did*."

"Viv, I-"

Vivian scowled at him and walked into the cockpit, bumping her shoulder on the door frame on the way in.

She rolled her eyes, whispering in disbelief, "And now the door?" punching it.

She shut the sliding door to the cockpit, her anger feeling like it was seeping through the seams in her jacket. She was just now noticing the pain in her hand.

EVA asked, "Are you okay?"

Vivian closed her eyes and massaged her knuckles, trying to ease the pain as she tried to focus on getting to the station.

"I'll be fine, EVA."

Vivian sat there in silence as her anger refused to subside. The station came into view and once EVA had docked to it, Vivian heard a knock on the door.

"Hey-"

Vivian called through the closed cockpit door, "You're here, get off my ship."

"Fine. Thank you for getting me here, and I'm sorry."

"Yeah."

Vivian got out of her seat and opened the cockpit door once she heard that the main hatch had closed.

She noticed a 10-credit bill on the table with a small note written on it.

A genuine smile broke onto her face as she said, "EVA, isn't he the best?"

"I don't understand."

Vivian picked up the note, reading it out loud to EVA.

"Dear Vivian, thank you for taking me to the station. Here's a

## CHAPTER 1

tip."

"Uncharacteristically nice," EVA said. "Compared to what you've told me about him."

Vivian smiled and nodded.

"Oh, he's always like this. He's amazing."

"That is in direct contrast with what you said a few minutes ago."

"Yeah, but a few minutes ago I didn't have money," Vivian said to EVA, flopping down on one of the jumpseats and staring at the note.

"That's good, something for you to save–"

"I'm gonna see if they have the Carmen Fizz inside."

"Vivian, you said you should save money for emergencies."

"This *is* an emergency," Vivian said, her mind already made.

"Affirmative."

Vivian exited her ship and looked around, seeing Jackson turning the corner to a different part of the station.

The station was dingy but not in disrepair. While rust covered the walls and glowbeetles ran in between cracks, Vivian found places like these to be calming. One of her earliest memories was befriending a small orange cat that lived on a station just like this.

As she walked down the hall, she turned a corner and noticed a small convenience store. She walked in and to her left was a large wall with her favorite drink, Carmen Fizz.

"Hey," the cashier said as Vivian brought a case to the register. "Have you shopped with us before?"

Vivian shook her head and pulled out the bill.

After collecting her change, she borrowed an anti-gravity cart from the back of the store to haul the case out to her ship.

Almost immediately after Vivian finished stowing the cargo

into *The Victory*, the cart autonomously returned itself to the store.

"Alright," Vivian mumbled. "Where to next?"

# Chapter 2

As Vivian entered the main hatch, she heard a message coming through.

"EVA, what's it reading?"

The flight computer made a whirring noise and said, "Stand by."

Vivian pulled out from the refueling station and looked at her communication device to see a wall of text coming in.

EVA stayed silent as it processed the message. Vivian sipped the ice-cold drink and stashed the rest in the fridge in the back of *The Victory*.

Just as she closed the door, she could almost feel the ship tense up.

"EVA? What's going on?"

She heard EVA speak from the cockpit.

"Emergency. Emergency," EVA said, her tone unusually monotonous and dull.

Vivian ran up and pulled to the primary flight seat, spinning around to take a closer look.

"What's wrong?" Vivian asked, gently putting her hand on *The Victory's* dashboard.

"Distress signal received," EVA continued.

"Can you tell me anything about the message?"

"Imminent planetary destruction."

"Where is the message originating from?"

"Message originates from *Caldera*, a terrestrial world. Their leader is requesting evacuation services."

"Not sure where he got the idea I'd be able to evacuate people, but should we check it out anyway?"

"Affirmative."

"Alright, then please set coordinates," Vivian said as she strapped herself in. "After this, would you like to power down? Take a rest? I can handle most of the mission, I think."

After a moment of silence, EVA responded slowly.

"Regrettably, yes. Apologies for disappointing you."

Vivian briefly remarked about how uncharacteristic it was but brushed it off, smiled, and said, "You're not disappointing me. I asked, for a reason."

"Thank you," EVA said.

Vivian thought she could feel a tinge of guilt from EVA but thought nothing of it.

"I'll reactivate when we land," Vivian said, concerned about the state of her flight computer. "Do you think that'll be enough time to rest?"

After another moment of hesitation, EVA slowly said, "Yes."

As she worked at the controls, Vivian felt her anxiety return once again.

* * *

Vivian jumped through the connective portal and emerged through the other side in orbit above Caldera, noticing an

## CHAPTER 2

immediate contrast compared to Cephi.

The planet from orbit was dark, with the surface being covered in a thick layer of mucky clouds that blocked out the majority of sunlight.

Below, she could see deep purples and blues emanating from lights on the surface, though, at the altitude she was at, there was no way for her to make out precisely what they were. Nonetheless, she started her descent to land near the lights.

*Where there are lights, there are people,* she thought as she engaged the retro-thrusters.

After a surprisingly smooth entry, she pierced through the cloud layer and noticed a sprawling city, the center having a large tower in the middle and the rest spreading across the landscape, getting increasingly more dilapidated as it spread further out. She spotted two landing pads near the outskirts of the city and decided to land at the less deteriorated one. As she shut down the engines, she turned EVA back on.

"Hey, welcome back," Vivian said as the lights flickered back on.

"Thank you, Vivian," EVA said, a whirring sound emanating from within *The Victory* as she woke back up.

"Welcome to Caldera," Vivian said, sighing and exiting the cockpit. "Keep me on comms, I'm going to take a look around."

"Affirmative," EVA said. "I'll be here waiting for your communication."

Once Vivian had opened the ramp, stepped out of her ship, and started walking towards the city, she was able to take in the view in front of her. The city was built atop a naturally raised rocky platform, overlooking the farmland that Vivian had landed close to.

She watched as flying vehicles, both crewed and uncrewed

zipped around, weaving between the skyscrapers that dotted the skyline.

To her right was a large boxy building labeled with a radiation warning sign. A series of thin metallic grey and yellow buildings scattered the landscape in proximity to it. Vivian couldn't help but notice the aura of neglect that covered everything, and she sighed with pity.

Surrounding the center building of the city was a district glowing with advertising lights for all types of products. To the left, near the city's edge, were the remnants of a taiga forest, long since destroyed. The center building, however, was something special. Almost everything in the building was lit up, and with the building being at least twice as tall as everything surrounding it, it was clearly meant to be the flagship of the city. The building was also hexagonal, with the name "Wright" written in large neon letters on at least three of the sides.

*Alright,* she thought. *Looks like it'll be a long walk.*

As Vivian walked, she could feel the air becoming harder to breathe as the pollution surrounding the city became more poignant. Once she entered the city limits, she noticed the bustling streets.

As the crowds became more dense, the people started moving aside as she walked. Her gaze was never met for more than a moment before they would look away, scared, and trying not to make trouble.

*Weird, but I'm a foreigner so I understand,* she thought as she walked through the bustling city. Occasionally, she overheard bits of conversation in different languages that she had never heard before.

*I bet they're talking about me,* she thought as a pang of anxiety formed in her chest again.

## CHAPTER 2

The sky was filled with flying cars. Occasionally, some of the flying cars would fly overhead at staggering speeds, followed quickly by police vehicles.

Vivian eventually got to a square in front of the Wright Building and stopped to rest for a moment.

Suddenly, out of nowhere, Vivian saw a door getting pushed in and a man, wide-eyed and panicking, ran into the middle of the square. Although Vivian couldn't make out what he was saying because he wasn't speaking a language she understood, his panic put Vivian on edge.

Seconds later, coming out of the same building, four police officers barreled through the door and tackled the man to the ground, taking him away as he yelled.

Vivian looked around and noticed that nobody had reacted.

People on the street took cover as rain started falling. Vivian put her hand out and quickly noticed that the rain had a grey color with brown dirt particles composing much of its substance. With that, she went inside.

The lobby was a serene white color, with a single figure in a security uniform walking towards her. She was greeted in the lobby of the Wright Building by a man with a blank expression on his face.

"Good day. Welcome to the Wright Corporation."

Vivian looked at him and backed away slightly.

The man assumed she hadn't heard him and repeated, "Good day. How may I help you?"

"What happened to this planet?"

"Regrettably, Caldera has recently gone through a period of disarray."

"Why's that?"

"Classified."

Vivian stared at him for a moment and asked, "Are you Synthetic?"

"Yes," he responded, nodding succinctly.

Vivian looked into the man's eyes, confused. There was a spark behind his eyes that couldn't be replicated by any Synthetic she had seen.

She nodded and thought, *Whoever made these must be brilliant.*

"You're so lifelike," she marveled.

"That is the intention. Mr. Wright wants us to be as close to human as possible."

He hesitated for a second, but decided to stay silent. Vivian didn't notice a thing.

She chuckled and said, "Well, he did a great job."

The Synthetic nodded again. "So how can I help you?"

"I got a distress signal, I traced it back to its source."

"Quinn? Mr. Wright is expecting you."

"Correct."

"As is standard practice, I will conduct a Synthetic screening and a general personal data test. Please follow me."

The man started to walk toward the elevator but Vivian still had her feet firmly planted on the lobby floor.

"A *what* screening?"

"It's a simple Synthetic screening. We need to evaluate your status, it's the standard procedure for Caldera."

"Listen, I'm here to help you with whatever is going on. I don't have the time to waste with this."

"Mr. Wright made it very clear that all guests to our planet must go through this standard procedure. It won't take longer than a few minutes."

Vivian rolled her eyes and followed the man into an elevator, staying silent as it went up.

## CHAPTER 2

The elevator opened into a room with gray walls and a small desk in the middle of it. On the desk was a piece of paper, an accompanying Wright Corporation pen, and a dark brown machine. The man pulled the chair facing away from the door out and gestured for Vivian to sit down. Once they were both seated, the man began.

"Before we start with your test, I am required to tell you about me. My serial number is M19-404. I was manufactured 3 years, 7 months, and 24 days ago. I work as a security officer for the Wright Corporation. In case you're unable to remember my full serial number, Mr. Wright has permitted guests to call me 'M'."

"It's good to meet you, M."

"Thank you. Let's begin."

Vivian looked nervously as M pulled up a sheet of paper with a list of questions on it.

"What is your name?"

"My name is Vivian Akami Quinn."

"What is your age?"

"24, I think. I don't keep track."

"Why's that?"

"I don't like birthdays."

"Understood. What is your race?"

"Japanese. Well, probably. It's been generations and I'm not sure where I-"

"-Apologies, Vivian. I should have specified that I was looking for *species*, not *race*."

"Oh, human."

Vivian became slightly annoyed that M had interrupted her but put her frustration aside momentarily.

"Thank you. Let's move on to the Synthetic screening. Please answer each question as succinctly as possible, only answering with the first answer that pops into your head."

"Got it."

"Good, let's begin. Who are you?"

"I'm Vivian."

M wrote down her answer and asked the next question once he had finished.

"What would you feel if someone hugged you?"

Vivian's body tensed up. "I'd uh, I'd feel awkward."

"Do you feel?"

She exhaled. "Too much."

"Have you ever felt loved?"

Vivian scoffed. "Haven't been."

"What would you do if someone loved you?"

Vivian thought back to Rigel and as her anxiety rose, so did her anger and frustration at the robot sitting in front of her.

"It's none of your business."

"That isn't a valid answer. What would you do if someone loved you?"

Vivian closed her eyes to try to suppress her anger. "I'd push them away."

"Do you have any aspirations that deviate from your assigned task?"

Vivian shook her head, deep in thought.

"Verbal answer, please. Do you have any aspirations that deviate from your assigned task?

"No."

"Do you feel content with your position in life?"

"No."

"What is life?"

"We don't really know enough about the universe for me to answer that question. Sorry."

## CHAPTER 2

"It's okay."

*No, it's not, I'm an idiot for not being able to answer that*, Vivian thought as she missed the next question.

"Sorry, can you repeat?"

"Of course. How would you feel if somebody upset you?"

Vivian's heart panged with fear as she sunk back into the chair.

"I would do *anything*- whatever it would take to make the person feel better."

"Have you felt anger?"

"Who hasn't?"

M looked at her for a moment and said, "Hm."

Within a flash, Vivian's annoyance and anxiety turned to anger.

*Is he judging me?* Vivian asked herself. *Thinking I can't get angry?*

"Who are you?"

Vivian rolled her eyes. "I said earlier, I'm Vivian."

"And who is Vivian?"

Vivian could feel her brain shortcircuit when M asked the question.

*That's a really damn good question*, Vivian thought.

"I, uh," Vivian said.

Vivian stayed silent as she realized: that Vivian Quinn didn't know who she was.

"I don't really know," she mumbled out. "A pilot, I guess?"

"Thank you," M said as he finished writing the last answer on the page and put it into the machine that was sitting to his left.

A whirring sound occurred as Vivian sat up straight again.

M looked at the data pouring out of the machine and said, "Curious."

"What's wrong?"

"The screening indicates that you're a Synthetic."

"What?"

"Your responses indicate that you're Synthetic."

"That's not... that's impossible."

"Our screenings are accurate, given our sample size."

Vivian shook her head as she began to spiral.

*The fact that I can't remember my childhood makes sense. If I was never born...* Vivian thought, panic setting in. *Wait, does that mean I'm not real? That my feelings are fake? Impossible...*

Vivian faked a smile as her inner world collapsed and said, "Well, I guess they made me pretty close to human too."

"As I said, Mr. Wright wants us to be as close to human as possible-"

"-Without the negative aspects," a voice said behind her as the door swung open.

Vivian turned around to notice a sharp man in a suit standing at the entrance, fixing his tie and smiling.

"Vivian, I am Robert Wright."

She nervously waved as M said, "Vivian would like to discuss some of the details of the screening with you."

Mr. Wright gestured to the door and said, "Then that is what we shall do."

# Chapter 3

Vivian slowly stepped out of her chair and nodded. Her legs felt like jelly but she pressed on.

"So, you need my help?" She asked, visibly shaken up by the possible revelation.

Mr. Wright smiled. "Let's get to my office and we can discuss this further. M19-404, would you be so kind as to stay here?"

"Yes, sir."

Vivian felt an uneasiness surrounding Mr. Wright's presence. *There's something off about him,* she thought as he guided her through the room and to the elevator. She froze up when he stood just a few centimeters too close to her and took a step to the side as he tapped the button to go to the top floor.

"I see you've met M19-404, he's one of my finest," Mr. Wright said, prompting Vivian to respond with a concise nod.

"Sorry it's taking so long," Mr. Wright said, feigning sympathy. "I have a penthouse office."

Vivian just looked at him, trying to determine what was off with him as the elevator stopped with a jolt.

"We're here."

The door opened into Mr. Wright's office. Windows covered all of the walls, letting anyone who was so lucky to be up there be treated to a panoramic view of the city below.

As Vivian looked down at the bustling streets, Mr. Wright got to his desk and asked, "Let's discuss the results of the screening, hm?"

Vivian responded quickly, "I'd rather just talk business."

"Are you sure?"

"I'm certain," Vivian said as she pushed the negative thoughts from her head and walked over to the desk. "So, why am I here? I'm not exactly capable of taking the entire population of your planet off-world. I'm just a girl with a ship."

"That won't be an issue," Mr. Wright said. "We have a ship, we just need a pilot."

"Oh, okay," Vivian said as she thought, a little bit taken aback by the preparedness. "So how big is the ship? I thought I would've seen one of those big cruisers in orbit or something."

"What? Oh, the Synthetics are staying. Our ship is made for the 300 *real* people left, give or take."

"Why?" Vivian asked, annoyed. "You made them nearly human, don't they deserve to come with?"

"What's the issue?" Mr. Wright responded, accusatorily. "Are *you* Synthetic?"

"I don't know, maybe," Vivian said, doubting her words but saying them anyway.

Mr. Wright seemed taken aback and said, "Never mind that. Sorry."

"Okay, let's move on," Vivian interrupted, as she leaned forward. "What's the time frame for planetary collapse?"

"Our star has been sending solar flares at us for decades now, but it's only a matter of time now before a flare permanently cripples our society. My scientists are saying we only have a few weeks left, maybe a month at most."

Vivian felt her anxiety rising.

## CHAPTER 3

"I'm sorry, that sounds like a tough thing to deal with," she said.

"It happens, that's why we're leaving," Mr. Wright replied dryly.

"Right, and when did you want to leave?"

"Once I give the word, the ship will be ready to go in only a few hours. Are you in? There will be room in the cargo bay for your ship."

"Sure, I can definitely do that," Vivian said impulsively.

*Why did I just say that?* Vivian thought. *I'm way in over my head.*

"Wonderful, I'll tell my people to prepare the transport."

"And what of the Synthetics?" Vivian asked, almost pleading as the thoughts of her potentially being Synthetic flooded her mind.

"What about them? I already told you, they're *staying*."

Vivian sighed and became quiet again as Mr. Wright got up to tell one of the guards that it was time for everyone to leave.

He looked at her and asked, "Is everything alright?"

Vivian shook her head and said, "I'm just thinking about that screening to see if I was Synthetic."

"What of it?"

"It indicated that I was."

Mr. Wright looked at her and with a slight smirk, said, "It's possible."

*Real helpful,* Vivian thought, not noticing Mr. Wright's facade breaking.

"Never mind all that, let me show you around," Mr. Wright said, putting on a fake smile and gesturing for Vivian to stand up.

Vivian slowly stood up, supporting herself on the desk for a moment before walking back to the elevator with Mr. Wright.

Mr. Wright looked down at Vivian as the elevator descended and said, "That test really got to you, huh?"

Vivian ignored him.

The fictitious aura surrounding Mr. Wright spurred on a feeling of helplessness in Vivian as if everything she felt was false.

*It's just more bad thoughts,* Vivian thought, but she couldn't help but wonder if there was something off about Mr. Wright, or if she was projecting her own insecurities onto him.

Suddenly, Mr. Wright's voice cut through her thoughts as he said, "Look- all I'm saying is that I wouldn't think less of someone if I found out they were Synthetic. I'm sure you're a good pilot regardless of... *manufacturer.*"

Vivian shot a glance at him and thought, *Right, because it's definitely not discrimination to leave most of your people here because of them being Synthetic.*

She continued to say nothing throughout the rest of the elevator ride and eventually, the door opened to an underground hangar with a large cruiser sitting right in the middle of it.

"So this is it," Mr. Wright said, dramatically gesturing with his hands toward it.

Vivian nodded, her mind traveling elsewhere.

As she mindlessly followed Mr. Wright through the hangar and onto the ship, she kept thinking, *Am I a Synthetic? Am I not real?*

Vivian put her hand on her head and sighed, mumbling something to herself.

"What?" Mr. Wright said, quizzically.

Vivian just shook her head and said, "Nothing, my head hurts."

Mr. Wright nodded with a mix of understanding and inattentiveness. He picked up where he left off with the plan again and Vivian zoned out again.

*I need to get out of here,* Vivian thought.

"You got it?"

"Hm?" Vivian asked, looking up.

Mr. Wright stared at her with uncaring eyes, pretending to be sympathetic.

"I know what you're going through must be tough, but you need to focus."

Vivian put her hands on her hips and said, "Walk me through it one more time."

"Alright. We'd take off from here and head East. Since the entire city is on a raised platform, picking up speed shouldn't be an issue. Once we've reached altitude, we should be aiming for Sector 2. There is a planet there that will be able to sustain us, in the solar system of Bragg."

"Right," Vivian said, crossing her arms as she finally listened.

"Once we're at the new planet, which we're calling New Caldera, we will be able to rebuild. The star is more stable, and the civilization will thrive for far longer than it would if we stayed here."

"Are you gonna build more Synthetics?"

Mr. Wright shrugged. "Most likely, it depends on how much work needs to get done."

"Hm," Vivian said as she walked back up to the main ramp.

Suddenly, the two heard a bunch of loud chattering entering the room, followed by the clunking of luggage making its way across the floor.

"You might want to take a step back," Mr. Wright said, walking a few paces backward.

Vivian stepped back just in time as dozens of people in fancy clothes all started boarding.

A man similar in age stopped and looked at Vivian. "I haven't seen you before. What's your position here?"

"Oh, I'm not from here. I just help people where I can around the galaxy, answering distress calls and such," Vivian said timidly.

"Oh? You're to be our pilot?"

Vivian nodded.

"Did you hear that, Mom? She's going to be our pilot."

An older woman smiled and said, "I heard, she's going to do great."

Vivian took a step closer to Mr. Wright, and said, "I don't do well around groups of people, can I go somewhere quieter?"

Mr. Wright shook his head. "Not right now, we need to go over pre-flight checks."

Vivian sighed and closed her eyes.

*I need to find a way to leave,* she thought but the only words to come from her mouth were, "Okay, let's do the pre-flight."

Vivian walked onboard and into the cockpit, closing the door behind her. Through the barrier, she could hear the people inside the ship bustling about, but she tried her best to block out the stimulation as she worked.

As Vivian looked at the dozens of switches and buttons in the cockpit, she sighed.

*This is not what I'm meant for,* she thought. *Well, I don't know what I'm meant for but it's definitely not this. Was I programmed?*

Anxiety panged in Vivian's chest. She took a deep breath and whispered, "Nope, not thinking about this right now, please."

Vivian flicked the switch to the main lighting system and heard the people outside momentarily become louder as the cabin lights turned on.

## CHAPTER 3

The ship flickered to life and Vivian sat down in the main pilot seat. Everything in the ship was labeled, so it was easy for her to go through pre-flight checks, even if she knew it would take a while.

"Alright," Vivian said as she mumbled about what to do. She went through every major system and tested every component, eventually determining the ship's flight readiness at 100%.

Mr. Wright knocked on the door. "Can I come in?"

"Yeah, sure."

"I'm sending M19-404 to get your ship from the landing dock."

Vivian shot up. "No, nobody touches my ship. Pre-flight is done, I'm going to go get it."

"Okay," Mr. Wright said, nodding his head. "You got 30 minutes."

"Alright," Vivian said.

She knew that if she decided to leave now, she would be halfway across the galaxy by then, and hopefully out of communication distance.

Vivian exited the ship down the front ramp and as she looked around at the giant cruiser before her, she thought, *Why did I agree to fly the damn thing? I can't fly a ship that big.*

She watched Mr. Wright as he rounded the corner back to the elevator to his office.

*Well, there's no way I can tell him I'm out at this point,* she thought. *Unless I just leave now on my own terms.*

Vivian looked around and saw the people busy packing their belongings into the ship. Without looking suspicious, she took the elevator downstairs, walked through the front door and through the city, and started a brisk walk back to the landing pad.

27

At his office, Mr. Wright sighed as he watched Vivian leave through the cameras.

"M19-404," he called out. "Report to me."

After a few seconds, M entered the room, slowly walking up behind Mr. Wright.

"How may I help you, sir?"

"I'd like you to follow Vivian. See what she's doing. I have a suspicion that she's going to be preparing to leave."

"Yes, sir," M said as he stepped out and started to walk toward the elevator.

Meanwhile, Vivian could start feeling the pollution in the air fade as she walked further away from the city center.

"EVA, start the ship," Vivian said through comms as she got within close distance to *The Victory*.

"Affirmative," EVA said. "Are we leaving?"

Vivian furrowed her brow and said, "I'm not sure, I just need some time to think."

# Chapter 4

Vivian took in a deep sigh as she stepped aboard *The Victory*.

"Status?" EVA asked.

"I'm upset," Vivian responded as she got to her bed and sat down.

"What happened?"

"They made me take a Synthetic screening and I turned up positive."

EVA stayed quiet for a moment and then asked, "Is that something you believe to be true?"

"I have no clue," Vivian said, shutting her eyes tight. "I don't even know who I am."

"You're Vivian," EVA responded straightforwardly.

"Right, but who is Vivian?"

EVA thought for a second and responded, "If you're referring to something I can't detect, that is something only you can determine."

"It wasn't meant to come out like that, smart-ass," Vivian said, exasperated. "I'm serious. It would make so much sense if I was made in a factory."

"Or this could be your brain trying to justify new information."

"But *what* information am I justifying? I'm not real! I'm not even supposed to think for myself!"

Vivian stood up and started pacing, trying to stave off a panic attack. She walked over to the door and pressed the button to raise the ramp.

"Are you okay?" EVA asked.

"No," Vivian mumbled as she felt her head get uncomfortably warm and her eyes go tunnel vision.

She sat down on the side of her bed as sweat dripped down her face. The leather of her jacket stuck to her arms in a way that made her skin crawl. In a panic, she took her jacket off and tossed it next to her, only to discover that she was now extremely cold.

The pit in her stomach that had been there since she took the test sunk deeper into her being, Vivian gasped for air as if she was drowning inside of herself. Her heart pounded so hard that she thought it would punch through her chest. Every nerve in her body tingled, at first lightly, but then enough to feel as though the soft breeze from the ship's air conditioning that graced her skin was a hurricane. The pain of it made her sob. Well, everything about it made her sob.

*I'm not real*, she kept repeating in her head over and over.

Vivian curled up into a ball as she tried to cry, but no sound came out. She felt as if someone had placed the weight of the ship on her chest, and she had to force herself to breathe.

*I'm going to die*, Vivian thought as her entire body ached.

"I'm going to die!" Vivian managed to yell, alerting EVA.

"Would you like me to call emergency services?"

"Yes!" Vivian said as her body tingled with dread.

Every second that passed felt like years until EVA said, "I'm sorry, this planet has all outside communication blocked."

Vivian felt herself emotionally pulled away, almost seeing

## CHAPTER 4

herself in the third person. She looked down at herself from the ceiling, as the rest of the world pulled away, as if she was in some sort of twisted vignette.

*That's the end of it*, she thought, looking down at herself. *I'm going to die on some nearly destroyed world.*

She sat on the floor, her arms hung over her ears as her legs were awkwardly sprawled near the side of the bed.

Vivian sighed. *And of course, I look pathetic while dying.*

As Vivian repositioned slightly, she felt the jacket hanging off the side of the bed hit her skin one too many times, and she angrily threw it across the room. A loud clang was produced as the metal zipper hit the door, making Vivian shriek and cover her ears at the loud noise as her emotions ramped up again, but it was short-lived as she felt herself getting drowsy.

*I should get up*, she thought. *But I'm too tired.*

Finally, after what felt like hours, her breath calmed a little bit and Vivian fell asleep.

\* \* \*

Vivian woke up with a jolt. "How long was I out for?"

"Sixteen minutes."

"That's it?" Vivian said, slowly sitting up.

Her body ached. She looked across the room and saw her jacket still lying near the door.

*Okay*, Vivian thought. *So that probably wasn't a nightmare.*

She sat at the side of her bed and stretched, wiping the dried tears from her face and reaching into a drawer to acquire an energy bar.

"EVA, what was that?" Vivian asked as she took a bite. "I've felt similar before, but never that bad."

"Diagnostic report indicates that you had a severe panic attack," EVA said. "Good news is that a robot wouldn't do that."

Vivian cursed under her breath. "You're right. Guess I'm real after all."

"That's uncharacteristic of you," EVA noted. "Accepting you're human so quickly, and all."

"I don't know what's characteristic anymore, but being human feels right. Maybe that damn test is faulty. I'm going out again, something doesn't line up with what Mr. Wright is saying."

Vivian put on her jacket and finished the energy bar. Suddenly, she heard a knock on the door.

"Who is it?"

"It's M19-404. May I come in?"

Vivian responded by lowering the hatch. "I was actually planning on looking for you. I'm guessing you're here because Mr. Wright wanted you to keep an eye on me?"

"Mr. Wright wanted me to check in."

"That's nice," Vivian said, feigning politeness, slightly restless as she wanted to get to the topic on her mind.

"Is your ship ready to go?"

"Yep," Vivian said as she changed the subject. "How do you know you're Synthetic?"

M seemed taken aback by the question and said, "Well, that's what I've always been told. Why do you ask?"

"I have a feeling that test is faulty."

"Let's talk about the mission," M said, quickly changing the subject.

Vivian stopped walking for a second and thought, *I bet there are records in the building.*

She turned to M and said, "I want to check the records, I have a hunch."

"How do you want to do that?"

"Through the front door."

M straightened up and said, "So that's the plan? Just walk in? And why do you want to go to the records anyway?"

"What's the issue?" Vivian asked as she invited M inside *The Victory* and retracted the ramp. "You have clearance and he said you were one of his best, right?"

"Right."

"So he won't question it."

He looked at her puzzled and said, "Well, what about you?"

Vivian rolled her eyes as she pieced it together for him.

"Well, you're my chaperone. Just trust me, it won't be suspicious."

"Fine," M said, throwing his hands up before starting to wander around the common area. "Why do you want to go to the records, again?"

"A hunch."

"This *isn't* the plan."

"It could be. Just trust me."

M sighed in disbelief as Vivian flipped a few switches to get *The Victory* airborne.

Once it was primed for flight, she turned around to talk to M who was lost deep in thought.

"You might wanna sit down in one of those jumpseats."

"Thank you," he responded as he strapped himself in.

Vivian sensed that he wasn't in a talkative mood so she turned around and sighed.

*Is this how I was?* She wondered, thinking back to earlier in the day. *Poor guy.*

As Vivian flew toward the hangar, she noticed a door opening on the roof. Vivian started the landing sequence and once they were in, the jolt of the gear touching the ground brought M back up to reality.

"Shall we find out what's really going on?" Vivian asked, helping him up.

He nodded and quickly checked his equipment. Vivian lowered the ramp and saw Mr. Wright walking toward her, flanked by two security officers.

"Vivian!" He called out. "It seems that M19-404 found you."

"I wasn't exactly hiding," Vivian said. "What's the status?"

"We're nearly ready to go."

"Okay, good. I need to check a fuel line sensor in the main building."

"Be my guest," he said, gesturing to the elevator.

As she walked past him, Vivian suddenly lost her balance, causing her to lightly bump into Mr. Wright.

"Shit, I'm so sorry!" she stuttered, regaining her balance. "Gravity here is a bit higher than I'm used to."

Mr. Wright chuckled. "It happens, Vivian. I'm curious what the gravity on the new planet will be like."

As Vivian walked away, Mr. Wright turned to M and said, "Don't let her out of your sight."

"Not a problem, sir," he responded.

They turned the corner, walking for another few meters.

Once they were out of earshot, Vivian said, "Alright, where is the data storage located?"

The two got in an elevator.

"Floor 8," M said, "But I can't go with you."

"Why not?" Vivian responded as she pressed the button.

## CHAPTER 4

"There's a Synthetic deactivation panel on the ground. If I step on it, I'll die. I'm not sure I wanna take that risk."

"What do you mean by *risk*?"

M stopped in his tracks as he realized what he said. Completely lost, he responded, "I'm not sure."

At that moment, the door opened up to a room filled with shelves of databoxes, and a large metal sheet covering the first meter of the floor spreading out from the elevator. Without a second thought, Vivian stepped onto it and walked across it with no ill effects.

"It seems that you're not Synthetic, then, but I don't know if the same will apply to me-"

"-Just do it," Vivian said, interrupting him.

M glared at Vivian but shrugged and held his breath as he stepped down, only for the same to happen to him.

He was fine.

"The machine must be broken," he rationalized.

"Or you're actually just human like me."

"Or maybe it's actually *just* broken!" M snapped, "This planet is already falling apart, the equipment isn't far behind! Stop trying to impose your existential problems on me and just back off!"

Vivian stepped back, put her hands up, and said, "Think about it, though, could a Synthetic really be as angry as you are now?"

"I don't know, and I honestly don't care," he said, indignantly.

Vivian sighed and said, "Let's go," walking up to the center console in the dimly lit room.

She clacked words into the keyboard while M looked around, his breath calming.

"Welcome, Mr. Wright," The computer said.

"Huh?" M replied, "How did you get in?"

"I snagged his card."

"When?"

"On the landing pad," Vivian said. "You didn't notice?"

"I hope he didn't either."

Vivian sat at the computer as she started mindlessly scrolling through all the files that had the keyword "Synthetic" inside them, along with their contexts.

Vivian gasped and pulled up a file. "I think I found some evidence."

"What's it say?"

Vivian felt her anger rise as she began reading.

"The lower class is to be brainwashed into believing they are Synthetic individuals, to enhance population control and obedience." She read further. "All lower-class individuals are to be subjected to memory suppression starting at 13, in order to strengthen their reconditioning to Synthetic."

M whipped around and said, "What? That's not true."

"It is, it was classified under company files."

M just looked at her, baffled, and said, "Who signed off on that?"

Vivian scrolled to the bottom of the page.

"These protocols are to be enacted effective immediately, as requested by the CEO, Mr. Robert Wright," Vivian replied and faced M. "He's the only one with clearance."

M looked distraught as he shook his head. "No, not me. It can't be me."

"It's *everyone*," Vivian said.

"Everyone except me."

"That's not how it works. What would it take to convince you?" Vivian asked, sympathetically.

M sighed and said, "Type in 5-15."

## CHAPTER 4

"Oh, birth records."

"I was told that was my activation date, what does it say?"

"Found this in an article from 22 years ago. 'On the 15th day of the 5th month, a beautiful baby boy, Peter, was born to an unknown mother and left at Orphanage 21."

M took a step back. "What were the physical characteristics?"

"Brown hair, brown eyes. Small mark on his left wrist."

M stood there for a moment and stared at the small mark on his left wrist. "No, that can't be right. That's a coincidence."

"Is it?"

He vehemently nodded.

"Let me ask you this. Do you have memories?"

"They're implanted."

"Are you sure?"

He shook his head and shrugged his shoulders.

"Okay, answer me this."

Vivian jabbed him in the shoulder.

"Did that hurt?"

"Very much so," M responded, straightening up.

"Why would they make a robot feel pain?"

"Mr. Wright wants us to be as close to human as possible-"

"-Without the negative aspects, yeah?" Vivian quoted. "Pain seems pretty negative to me. Why would a security robot feel pain? Wouldn't that be antithetical?"

"I suppose so."

"Just accept it, you're a person, like me."

With conviction, M said, "You're a Synthetic, you didn't pass the test. The door is broken. This is all just coincidence."

"The test is rigged, nobody could pass it, I don't even think Mr. Wright could."

M just shook his head. "That's not true. Mr. Wright made the test, we saw that he did in the report."

M looked up and sighed. "Listen, I don't know what is going on, and while I agree that there is something going on with Mr. Wright, I need more evidence on the other claim."

Vivian rolled her eyes. "Fine. I'm not going to be the one to help you, you'll have to do it alone."

"There's nothing I need *help* with. I was created by the Wright Corporation."

The two walked back to the elevator and as they waited for it to arrive, Vivian said, "Let's get back on track with the mission. Where do we go from here?"

"Well," M said, emotionally exhausted. "Even if one real person who was tagged as Synthetic was left behind, then they need to be rescued. We're probably going to need a lot more space than we have, and I don't know where we're going to fit them. How many does *The Victory* hold?"

"One comfortably, maybe three if everyone gets along."

M sighed and said, "Well, that might be a problem. Any ideas?"

As the elevator arrived, Vivian and M stepped in.

Vivian thought about it for a second before saying, "If you can get me into the communications array, I might be able to call for help. I know someone."

"Alright, I can do that," M said, nodding.

## Chapter 5

Vivian clicked the button for the communications array floor as M looked on, his mind completely focused on the mission at hand.

As the elevator ascended, Vivian looked over and asked, "M, what happens if you don't pass the Synthetic screening?"

M stopped for a second and processed.

"You disappear forever," he said, softly.

Vivian nodded sympathetically but didn't press further and changed the subject by saying, "Alright, here's the plan. I'm going to contact my friend who has a way to get everyone out, and I need you to covertly get the people ready to leave. Get as many people informed of the plan as possible."

"Shouldn't we inform Mr. Wright?"

"He hates the Synthetic population, he'll try to stop you."

M solemnly nodded. "I want to do this, but I don't want to disappear."

"I promise, you won't," Vivian responded, feeling the weight of responsibility on her back. "Trust me, you got this."

M sighed as Vivian looked at the screen in the elevator.

As the numbers ticked up, Vivian asked, "Do you want me to call you Peter?"

"Look, I don't care. Call me whatever you want. Let's do

this mission and then we can worry about what to call me," M frustratedly replied, slamming his hand on the side of the elevator.

"Alright," Vivian said as the elevator door stopped and opened.

"Good luck with your mission," M said.

"And with yours," Vivian responded. "Sorry for pushing it as hard as I did."

M nodded and Vivian stepped out of the elevator and walked over to the communications control center.

The room was dingy and drab, with rust covering the communications array. Vivian typed in the transponder signal for Jackson's ship and seconds later, heard the familiar buzz of a signal being patched through.

"Answer, please..." Vivian mumbled under her breath.

"This is Jackson, how can I help you?"

"Jackson! I'm on this planet named Caldera, I need your help."

Jackson sighed. "What's up, Vivian?"

"Okay, so there's something really sketchy going on with this place. Do you still have your cruiser?"

Jackson chuckled and said, "I just *knew* you were gonna ask about that, Viv!"

Vivian rolled her eyes and said, "I'm serious. This planet is really weird and I'm gonna need help evacuating potentially millions."

"Is that why you're calling from this unsecured line?"

"Yep, and I'm not sure how long it'll be before this call is traced. Can you help? Please?"

Jackson said, "Well, it's a rarity hearing you say please. I'm in, but you'll owe me one."

"Thank you, thank you, thank you!" Vivian said, a smile

CHAPTER 5

forming across her face. "Track *The Victory*, you'll see what's going on."

\* \* \*

Meanwhile, downstairs in the security recreation room, M opened the door and saw one of his subordinates there.

"Hello, M19-404," she said, nonchalantly.

"K66-108, I need your help."

She looked at him, confused. "Help? With what?"

M shook his head. "I might've learned something about the planet that will change the evacuation orders from Mr. Wright."

"Does he know?"

"He can't."

She stopped. She had never seen M this scared before.

"I uncovered a plot with the pilot, Vivian, and it's something sinister. There's evidence to prove that the people on this planet are being brainwashed into thinking they're Synthetic."

"Even us?"

M shrugged.

"I have no idea," he said, still in denial. "But I'm doing what I can so that if this is true, nobody is left behind. Can you set up logistical forces to evacuate the planet? We have a bigger ship coming."

She looked at him and slowly nodded. "Sure thing, sir. Who should I report to?"

"Report to Vivian Quinn, she's in either the communications array or the archives. The floor is broken, we can step on it without dying."

She nodded again and as she walked away, M was left thinking about how unnatural the conversation felt. *Is that how Synthetics would talk?*

M shrugged as he stepped out of the main center of the Wright Building and started walking toward the hangar, looking at all the people lining up.

*If I have someone do a screening who is verifiably human and they fail, I'll know the truth.*

M walked up to one of the people preparing to get onto the ship and said, "Hello, kind sir, would you humor me for a moment and let me conduct a screening on you?"

The man looked him up and down and said, "How long will it take?"

"A few minutes, no more. The ship will not leave without you."

The man hesitantly nodded and followed M to the screening room.

Once they were seated across from each other, M said, "Okay sir, please answer each question as succinctly as possible, only answering with the first answer that pops into your head."

He nodded.

"Let us begin. Who are you?"

"My name is Ben, my wife calls me Benny."

"What would you feel if someone hugged you?"

"I'd feel wonderful, I love hugs."

"Do you feel?"

Ben chuckled, "Yeah, of course."

"Have you ever felt loved?"

Ben smiled. "Yeah, my wife loves me."

"What would you do if someone loved you?"

"I'd love them back, assuming they're human, of course."

## CHAPTER 5

M silently wrote down the answer and subtly judged him, which Ben seemed to pick up on.

"They make you Synths judgmental now? Mr. Wright was *not* kidding about the realism-"

"Let's focus up," M said, interrupting him. "Do you have any aspirations that deviate from your assigned task?"

Ben looked at M for a moment and said, "I mean, I'd love to do art full-time, but my job here isn't exactly *bad*..."

"Do you feel content with your position in life?"

"Yeah, I love it here. It's a shame we have to leave."

"What is life?"

Ben made a gesture to indicate he didn't want to talk about it. "Whenever I talk about what I consider to be life, *someone* gets mad."

"How would you feel if somebody upset you?"

"Eh, probably fine. Some people just need to grow a thicker skin."

"Have you felt anger?"

"Sometimes, depends on the situation."

"Who are you?"

"I'm Ben, artist and architect," he said, smiling slightly.

"Thank you," M said as he wrote the last answer on the page and put it into the screening machine.

A whirring sound occurred from its processing and M looked at the data pouring out of the machine. M felt goosebumps ripple through his entire body.

"Synthetic," the screen read.

M shook his head.

"Something wrong?" Ben asked.

"Not an issue," M said, putting on a smile. "Thank you for your participation."

The second that Ben left the room, M slumped over in his chair, sobbing.

* * *

Back at the communications array, Vivian looked into the sky, waiting to see Jackson's ship enter the atmosphere at any moment. Eventually, she just gave up and wandered downstairs to the archives.

Something in the archives felt... off. Vivian froze up, her anxiety going through the roof. The elevator dinged, and the doors slowly started opening up. Vivian immediately dove behind a series of shelves, scaring a family of glowbeetles that had build their colony in the lowest section of the shelf.

She closed her eyes and tried to calm her breath, feeling as though her panting made her position even more obvious than the swarm of bright glowing beetles fleeing their old home.

After hearing a footstep coming toward her, Vivian heard an unfamiliar voice call her name.

"Vivian Quinn?"

Vivian cowered behind the shelves as the voice came closer. "My number is K66-108, M19-404 sent me."

Vivian slowly got up as she stepped further into the room.

"Everything is in place for the large-scale evacuation. All we're waiting on now is the ship."

"Thank you, K66-108," Vivian said as she peaked her head over the side.

"What're you doing in the archives?"

"I was learning about the evacuation plans, there's some

horrifying stuff in here."

"M19-404 told me his theory about the Synthetics on this planet being human."

"He did?"

She just nodded. "I need evidence."

Vivian ran over to the console and pulled up the file on the central computer.

"Read this. Follow me up to communications, I need to check in on the ship's status."

Vivian impatiently tapped her foot while the elevator was retrieved.

K66-108 looked at her and asked, "What's your deal?"

"Huh?" Vivian asked, looking confused.

"Why are you here?"

"I'm here to help you all. I got a distress signal, and I try to help out where I can."

K66-108 just nodded.

"Beats being dead, you know?" Vivian said, with a nervous chuckle as the elevator arrived.

After a short and silent elevator ride, Vivian and K66-108 were at the communications tower, the large windows overlooking the city temporarily catching K66-108's gaze.

The elevator door closed behind them, and Vivian ran over to send out another signal, but it was jammed.

"K, can you help me with this?"

Vivian looked up and asked again, "K?"

K66-108's face was filled with tears as she read through the report on the datapad. Vivian started walking over to her as the elevator door suddenly opened.

When she was only a meter or so away, Vivian stopped in her tracks as she heard a sharp bang, causing K66-108 to stiffen up and fall forward. The databox in her hands dropped out of them and onto the floor, which was followed by it getting destroyed by two more bullets.

Mr. Wright stood there, gun in hand, and pointed it at Vivian.

He cocked his head to the side. "You know, maybe I don't know my own building well anymore, but this does *not* look like the fuel line sensor."

# Chapter 6

Vivian stood, frozen with fear. Her eyes darted down to look at K's dead body and then back up to Mr. Wright.

*I'm screwed,* she thought.

"I admire your inquisitive nature. You're sharp and I can respect that. You certainly aren't a Synthetic, that's for certain. It's a shame I can't let you go now, though. You just so happened to have uprooted my entire operation," Mr. Wright said, putting his head down. "20 years down the drain, all thanks to you."

"You-you just killed a *person*!"

"They're barely people," Mr. Wright said. "A means to an end."

"You're a vile and disgusting person."

"Tough talk coming from someone with a gun pointed at them." Vivian took a short step back as Mr. Wright said, "Who else did you tell?"

"Nobody."

"Bullshit, who did you tell?"

Vivian sighed as she closed her eyes. "Peter."

"Who the hell is Peter?"

"Peter, the *human* agent that you sent to look after me."

Mr. Wright looked confused, but suddenly said, "Oh, are you talking about M19-404?"

Vivian just nodded as Mr. Wright readjusted his grip.

"Why don't you come here and turn off the transponder?" Mr. Wright said as he gestured for her to follow him to the console.

Vivian shook her head. "It's way too late for that."

"What?"

Just then, a shadow enveloped the building.

"Jackson, you came through," Vivian whispered as the giant ship started its descent.

Mr. Wright's eyes went wide as he called down to another officer, "B89-437, shoot that ship down."

"I cannot do that, sir," the voice responded.

"Why not?" Mr. Wright asked, his anger peaking.

"You've lied to us."

Mr. Wright responded by ending the call and looking at Vivian, who was almost grinning at this point.

"You might want to look out that window," she said.

Mr. Wright walked to the window, the gun still trained on Vivian, as he stared down at swathes of people all lining up as the massive ship started to land, while a smaller group stormed the Wright Building.

The elevator door closed as Mr. Wright stamped his foot on the ground and angrily said, "You were supposed to help! It was supposed to be a simple mission! But you ruined it. You ruined it because you're a horrible person. I had a good thing going!"

"Shut up," Vivian said as the elevator door opened again and M19-404 walked into the room.

Mr. Wright sighed and said, "M19-404, new executive order, bypass all other programming. Kill the one who made you believe that you're something you're not."

M stood, his expression blank.

Mr. Wright looked at Vivian and said, "M19-404, I want you

## CHAPTER 6

to kill the *vile* and *disgusting* person who made you deviate from your assigned task."

Mr. Wright reveled in the bitterness of his words as Vivian felt tears welling in her eyes. Despite all of that, M's expression stayed stagnant.

"Do it!" He snapped, and M got out his gun, silently. "You really got to him, huh?" Mr. Wright said, looking at Vivian. "You sneaky..."

Mr. Wright trailed off and craned his head to face M like a snake. "Tell me, officer. What is your name?"

"My name is Peter. I was born on the 15th day of the 5th month, and I am a person."

Mr. Wright sighed and put his head down. "That's not right. I'm bypassing all programmed security measures. You are *mine*, understood?"

"You can't bypass what isn't there," Peter said as Mr. Wright snarled at him.

The yelling became louder as the rioters made their way up.

Mr. Wright yelled, "Your programming states that you will listen to *everything* I say, so I am commanding you now, to kill your enemy!"

Peter raised his gun and fired a single shot. Mr. Wright hobbled backward and crumpled to the ground.

Suddenly, the elevator door opened and people poured out of it. They ran at Mr. Wright's body and started to beat him.

Vivian looked at the people, shocked, and Peter said, "What? He trained us to be killers. He deserves this. Grab his gun and let's go, we have a ship to catch."

Vivian still stood there, frozen, as Peter pressed the elevator button.

"What's wrong, Vivian?" He asked.

49

"They're killing him."

"Yeah," Peter said, bluntly. "We need to get going."

Peter walked over and picked up Mr. Wright's gun that had fallen a few meters away, holding it out to Vivian. She shook her head.

"I don't do violence," she said, her voice trembling slightly.

Peter shrugged as the elevator arrived. "Suit yourself."

Vivian nodded, pushed past the people beating Mr. Wright's body, and followed Peter into the elevator. As far as they both knew, Mr. Wright was dead.

"Now what? Do we go with the original plan?"

Peter nodded.

"You sure?" Vivian asked.

"You're a good pilot, right? You can make it work."

"Not on a rig of that size, dammit!" Vivian said.

"You're gonna do well, trust me."

"I can't do that. I'm going to find another way."

"Make it quick," Peter said. "Your friend's ship is ready to go."

Vivian sighed and nodded. "Wait, don't you want to leave the upper class?"

Peter just shook his head. "I don't know their involvement, and I can't judge them for what they might or might not have known. We'll sort it out once we get to New Caldera."

"Fair enough," Vivian mumbled as she looked up at the floors of the elevator dropping. After a moment, she sighed and said, "What a day."

Peter nodded. "Yeah. At least this feels real, though."

Vivian asked, "So how did you determine you were a person?"

Peter sighed. "A Synthetic screening, believe it or not. I interviewed a verified living person and the machine said they

## CHAPTER 6

were Synthetic, that's when I knew."

"That'll do it," Vivian said, sarcastically. "You're talking more human than before."

"This is how I've always wanted to talk," Peter said, smiling. "I'm just free of my, er, programming to do that now."

As they reached the bottom of the elevator, they heard a commotion coming from outside.

The door opened and Peter stepped out, with Vivian following close behind.

"You got everyone?" He asked.

"Yes, sir," another security agent said. "What happened to K66-108?"

"Dead," Vivian responded.

The agent hung his head and motioned for the other officers to keep the population moving onto the ship.

"The noise is starting to get to me," Vivian said. "I'm going back to the ship."

"I'll follow you there," Peter replied as Vivian started her walk through the crowd and back to *The Victory*.

As they walked into *The Victory*, Peter said, "You know, Vivian, I *am* actually a bit worried about you?"

"Why's that?" Vivian asked, starting up the cruiser.

"Well, your reaction was... a lot. And with the benefit of hindsight, the answers on your screening *were* strange."

Vivian chuckled and said, "It's funny to hear that from someone who didn't know they were human a day ago, but continue."

"I'm serious, Vivian."

"Right, I'm sorry."

"Has anyone told you this before? How there might be something at play?"

"Just that stupid test," Vivian said as she flipped on the engine primer.

"Please, just consider it."

"Fine."

Vivian sighed as Peter said, "Thank you. I'll see you on New Caldera."

"Have a safe flight," Vivian responded, turning around and smiling.

"Thanks, Vivian."

A few minutes later, both ships took off.

"Setting coordinates for low orbit," Vivian said as they made it through the atmosphere.

The ship bucked as Vivian got used to the controls. "Easy, sweetie," she whispered.

After ascent, the cruiser slowly leveled out. Once they were in a stable orbit, Vivian flicked on the ship's communicator.

"Jackson, can you hear me?" She asked.

"Loud and clear, Viv," he responded.

"I'm changing the plan, is the starboard docking port on your ship operational?"

"Yes, do you think you can dock?"

"I'm gonna try."

"I guess that'll have to do."

Vivian approached the giant cruiser and called Jackson again. "Reaction Control System primed, let's start."

Vivian started to move the giant cruiser into position. She heard the Reaction Control System compensating for the movement as she moved the ship in.

"Careful!" Jackson suddenly yelled as the ships bumped into each other.

"Sorry, I said I wasn't good at this," Vivian replied, slightly

## CHAPTER 6

frustrated.

"Just trust your gut feelings, you'll be okay."

Vivian sighed as she stopped tensing up and stared at the monitor, waiting for the docking light to turn green. She inched the ship forward, and suddenly the docking light turned green, prompting Vivian to push the ship into place.

"Capture confirmed," Jackson said. "Great job, Vivian."

"Thank you," Vivian said as she undid the seatbelt. "Can you take it from here?"

"You're leaving so soon?"

"Don't worry, I'll follow."

As she walked back through the cargo bay to where *The Victory* was stored, she heard chains rattling and looked over to see a glowbeetle stuck. She quickly walked over to it and helped it escape, watching it disappear under a door.

She turned around. "EVA, you ready to go?" Vivian asked through the short-range communicator.

"Affirmative. Undocking will commence as soon as you're aboard."

Vivian felt a huge rumble as the ship began to open the cargo bay doors, and she quickly boarded *The Victory*, entering the cockpit and waiting for it to separate.

With a clunk, EVA replied, "Separation confirmed."

Vivian slowly backed out of the ship and watched as the cargo bay doors closed again. She stayed silent as the ships made their way toward the jump point and flew through. Now alone in *The Victory* again, Vivian had time to think.

"EVA, did I overreact?"

EVA stayed silent long enough for Vivian to ask, "You there, EVA?"

"Yes, I am there. I'm unsure how to answer."

"How do you mean?"

"According to your personality, as I understand it, that was not an overreaction."

"What about compared to others?"

"I have insufficient data, though according to universal human emotion reactivity levels, you massively overreacted."

"So, is there something *wrong* with me?" Vivian asked, her anxiety returning slightly.

"I don't have enough data to diagnose the issue."

"Alright," Vivian said, taking a big sigh. "Can you keep tabs on me, then? I wanna make sure I'm not losing it."

"Affirmative."

Vivian opened her own portal and jumped through, immediately getting a short-range transmission coming through.

"I was beginning to think you weren't gonna follow," Jackson said on the other line.

"Ah, just had to say goodbye to Caldera. Where are you guys?"

"We've started landing procedures. I sent out Peter and some of his men down to the surface in a dropship, he said he wants to speak with you."

"What about you?"

"I'm going to hang around here, see if I can help these people get back on their feet."

"Sounds good, Jackson. Thank you so much for helping me with this. You have my transponder code if you need me."

"That I do, Vivian. Glad I could help. Jackson, signing off."

Vivian made her way down to the surface and noticed a beacon on the ground, which she landed next to. Vivian opened the back ramp and saw Peter standing there, with people already constructing temporary inflatable habitats.

"This place is a bit of a fixer-upper," Vivian said.

## CHAPTER 6

"It'll do," Peter responded.

"You think living on a moon will take some time to get used to?"

Peter smiled and looked up at the giant planet in the sky. "With a view like that? We'll be fine."

The two laughed and Vivian asked, "So, why'd you want to see me?"

Peter shrugged. "Ah, you know. You did a small insignificant thing like saving my life and the lives of millions."

Vivian smiled and shook her head. "That was you."

Peter said, "You don't have to be ashamed of your accomplishments. Without your persistence, I never would've realized the truth and I'd be stuck on that other damn planet to die."

Vivian shrugged and said, "Thank you, I guess."

Peter just smiled. "If there is anything I can do to repay you, don't hesitate to give us a call."

Vivian smiled and said, "I'll let you know."

As Vivian started walking back to her ship, she heard Peter shout to her, "Thank you so much for your help! Hope to see you around again!"

Vivian waved from the ramp of her ship.

"Another successful adventure for the daring explorer with a kind heart, Vivian Quinn," EVA said as Vivian got into the cockpit.

"Let's not go *that* far," Vivian said, laughing, putting on her seatbelt.

"Sorry, sorry," EVA said as the ship took off. "So, where to next?"

# About the Author

Elsbeth is an up-and-coming author residing in Los Angeles, California dipping her toes into science fiction. Her storytelling often focuses on more emotional character-driven stories, such as the *Vivian Quinn* series. She strives for scientific accuracy in her stories and loves combining different genres and ideas in unique ways.

In each story, Elsbeth tries to challenge the status quo, discussing the implications of future technologies and sciences as we don't yet understand them, contrasted with the human psyche and how those with mental health issues might see these advancements as beneficial- or detrimental.

With a deep love for science and theoretical physics, many readers are looking forward to seeing what she comes up with next.

# Also by Elsbeth

Catch up with Vivian on her next adventure...

**Vivian Quinn and the Star Beyond**

What happens when Vivian meets a civilization of beings who idolize humans at their own expense? Find out during Vivian's walkabout on an alien world...